For Mark
— C·A·

First published in Great Britain in 2012 by
Gullane Children's Books
185 Fleet Street, London EC4A 2HS
www.gullanebooks.com

Text and illustrations © 2012 Claire Alexander

This edition published in 2012 by Eerdmans Books for Young Readers,
an imprint of Wm. B. Eerdmans Publishing Co.
2140 Oak Industrial Dr. NE, Grand Rapids, Michigan 49505
P.O. Box 163, Cambridge CB3 9PU U.K.

www.eerdmans.com/youngreaders

Manufactured at Imago, in China, March 2012, first edition

12 13 14 15 16 17 18   8 7 6 5 4 3 2 1

ISBN 978-0-8028-5414-8

A catalog record of this book is available from the Library of Congress.

Back to Front
AND
Upside Down!

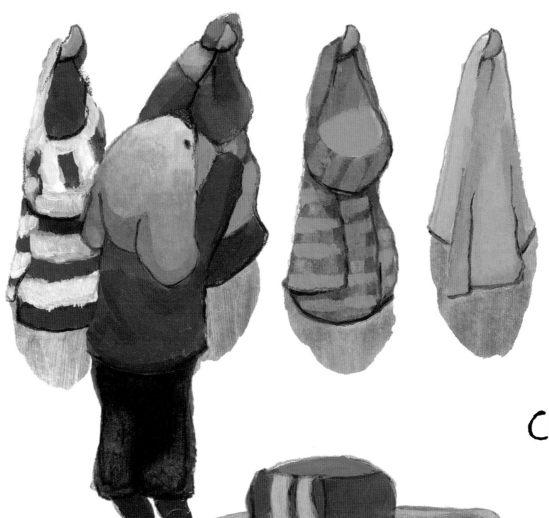

Claire Alexander

Eerdmans Books for Young Readers
Grand Rapids, Michigan • Cambridge, U.K.

One day during story time, the principal, Mr. Slippers, burst into Stan's classroom.

"It's my birthday," he boomed, "and I'm inviting you all to a special party this afternoon!"

Everyone was very excited.

When he was gone, Miss Catnip said,

"Let's all make **birthday cards** for Mr. Slippers!"

Stan had lots of brilliant ideas for what to draw.
"Excellent!" said Miss Catnip. "But first of all..."

"Your cards need to say **Happy Birthday**,"
she said, and wrote it up on the board.

Oh no! thought Stan.
He hadn't realized there would be writing!

Stan stared hard at the board.
He picked up his pencil and, very carefully,
he started to write . . .

But his letters came out back to front and upside down,
and some didn't look like letters at all!
I can't do it! Stan thought.

Miss Catnip was writing more words on the board. **To Mr. Slippers,** she read out.

That was really hard! Stan looked at Jack. He was busy writing his card.

He looked at Lucy. She was writing her card too.

Tommy had finished
and was writing
his name!

Stan's paws began to sweat
and his heart pounded loudly in his chest.

He wanted to ask Miss Catnip for help.
But everyone will laugh at me, he thought.

Stan felt sick, like his tummy was being all stirred up with a big wooden spoon.

Even his name was coming out in a muddle.

At recess
Stan didn't feel like playing.
He tried hard not to cry.
"Why are you sad?" asked Jack.

"Promise you won't tell?" said Stan.
Jack nodded, and Stan showed him his
back-to-front, upside-down letters.

"I'm the only one who can't do it!"
he said, and a big tear rolled
down his cheek.

"Don't cry, Stan," said Jack.
"Have you asked Miss Catnip for help?"

"I can't!" said Stan.
"Everyone will laugh at me!"

"No, they won't!" said Jack.
"We all have to ask for help sometimes."

After recess, Stan felt braver.
He took a deep breath and
asked Miss Catnip for help.

No one laughed at him.

"I'm glad you told me, Stan,"
said Miss Catnip.

"I'm having trouble too, Miss Catnip," said Mimi.

So Miss Catnip gently showed them what to do.

And after lots...

and lots...

and LOTS of practice...

more and more of their letters came out

the right way round and the right way up!

"Excellent!" said Miss Catnip.

Stan felt happy and proud of himself.
He couldn't wait to give his card to Mr. Slippers.

"Happy birthday, Mr. Slippers!" said Stan.

"Wow! What a great picture!"
exclaimed Mr. Slippers.

"Look inside!" cried Stan.

"I wrote it all myself!"

"Wonderful work!" declared Mr. Slippers,
as everyone began to sing
"Happy Birthday." Stan joined
in and sang at the top
of his voice.

Now Stan enjoys writing.

Sometimes it takes him longer
than everyone else, but when
he gets stuck, he **ALWAYS** asks
Miss Catnip for help.

So does Mimi . . .

well, most of the time!